A Beginning-to-Read Book

Astro the Alien
Visits Desert Animals

by Emily Sohn

Illustrated by Carlos Aón

NORWOOD HOUSE PRESS

DEAR CAREGIVER,

Books in the Beginning-to-Read collection are carefully written to develop the skills of early readers. The *Astro the Alien* series is a step up from the introductory *Dear Dragon* series. It provides early readers the opportunity to learn about the world through the narrative while building on their previous reading skills. The text in these books is comprised of common sight words and content words to expand your child's vocabulary. Increasing readers' sight word recognition promotes their reading fluency. The vivid pictures are an opportunity for readers to interact with the text and increase their understanding.

Begin by reading the story as your child follows along. Then let your child read familiar words. As your child practices with the text, you will notice improved accuracy, rate, and expression until he or she is able to read the story independently. Praising your child's efforts will build his or her confidence as an independent reader. Discussing the pictures will help your child make connections between the story and his or her own life. Reinforce literacy using the activities at the back of the book to support your child's reading comprehension, reading fluency, and oral language skills.

Above all, encourage your child to have fun with the reading experience!

Marla Conn, MS, Ed., Literacy Consultant

Norwood House Press • P.O. Box 316598 • Chicago, Illinois 60631

For more information about Norwood House Press please visit our website at www.norwoodhousepress.com or call 866-565-2900.

© 2019 Norwood House Press. Beginning-to-Read™ is a trademark of Norwood House Press.

Library of Congress Cataloging-in-Publication Data

Names: Sohn, Emily, author.
Title: Astro the Alien visits desert animals / by Emily Sohn.
Description: Chicago, Illinois : Norwood House Press, [2018] | Series: Beginning-to-read | Summary: "Astro the Alien and his friends Ben and Eva visit and learn about desert animals, including lizards, birds, and spiders. Includes reading activities and a word list"-- Provided by publisher.
Identifiers: LCCN 2018005657 (print) | LCCN 2018013280 (ebook) | ISBN 9781684041923 (ebook) | ISBN 9781599539201 (hardcover : alk. paper) | ISBN 9781684041855 (pbk. : alk. paper)
Subjects: | CYAC: Desert animals--Fiction. | Extraterrestrial beings--Fiction.
Classification: LCC PZ7.1.S662 (ebook) | LCC PZ7.1.S662 Asm 2018 (print) | DDC [E]--dc23
LC record available at https://lccn.loc.gov/2018005657

Hardcover ISBN: 978-1-59953-920-1   Paperback ISBN: 978-1-68404-185-5
312N—072018
Manufactured in the United States of America in North Mankato, Minnesota.

"Good morning, Astro!" said Ben.

"Are you ready to go camping?" asked Eva.

"Ready!" said Astro. "I'd like to see some desert animals."

"This is the desert, Astro," said Ben.

"Camping here is fun," said Eva.

"The desert is dry," said Eva. "It does not rain a lot. It can get hot!"

"Sometimes when it rains, it floods," said Ben.

"That is a Gila monster," said Ben.

"A monster?" asked Astro.

"Not a real monster," said Eva.
"It is a lizard."

"That is a rattlesnake," said Eva.

"Can we play with it?" asked Astro. "Rattles are fun!"

"No," said Ben. "We should leave it alone. If it is scared it might bite."

"Look at the dung beetles," said Eva. "Many insects live in the desert."

"I see a butterfly," said Ben.
"It is an insect, too."

"Pretty!" said Astro.

"Will we see a spider?" asked Astro. "I am afraid of spiders."

"Don't worry, Astro," said Eva. "We will watch for them."

"That bird is loud," said Astro.

"It is a cactus wren," said Eva.
"It builds its nest in the cactus."

"I see a toad and a tortoise," said Ben. "They stay warm in the sun."

"There is packrat," said Eva.
"It found something."

"And look. A roadrunner!" said Ben.

"It is so fast," said Astro.

"It is raining," said Astro.

"The river is rising fast," said Ben.

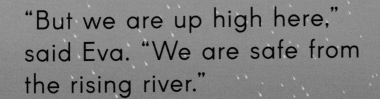

"But we are up high here," said Eva. "We are safe from the rising river."

"The rain stopped," said Astro.
"It is getting dark."

"Some animals come out at dawn and dusk," said Ben. "Over there! It's a bobcat."

"I see a jackrabbit, a mule deer, and a cottontail," said Eva.

"I hear a coyote," said Eva.

"I hear an owl," said Ben.
"They hunt at night."

"We saw a lot of animals today," said Eva.

"We heard a lot of animals, too," said Ben.

"We did not see a spider," said Astro. "Phew."

"There is a spider," said Ben.

"Oh, no!" said Astro.

"It is a tarantula," said Eva.
"It will not hurt you."

"We had fun seeing desert animals with you!" said Ben and Eva.

"The desert was exciting," said Astro. "Even the spiders!"

Comprehension Strategy

To check your child's understanding of the book, recreate the following sequence of events diagram on a sheet of paper. After your child reads the book, ask him or her to fill in the rectangles with animals or events that the kids and Astro encountered as they hiked up a mountain in the desert. Try to fill in six things they saw or did during their day.

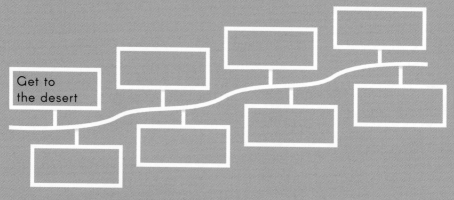

Get to the desert

Words

Vocabulary Lesson

Content words are words that are specific to a particular topic. All of the content words for this book can be found on page 32. Use some or all of these content words to complete one or more of the following activities:

- There are lots of animals in this book. Ask your child to group animal content words in two or three different ways.
- Have your child find content words that describe the environment in some way.
- Challenge your child to pick an animal from the book and draw it.
- Have your child identify words that are hard to spell. Can they write the words without looking at the book?
- Name a few characteristics that describe one of the content words. See if your child can guess the word.

Close Reading

Close reading helps children comprehend text. It includes reading a text, discussing it with others, and answering questions about it. Use these questions to discuss this book with your child:

- Why does Ben say they should leave some of the animals alone?
- Astro is afraid of spiders. Are there any animals that make you feel scared?
- What do you think makes some animals afraid of people?
- Have your child look around the house or library for other books or magazines that show pictures of animals in this book.

Foundational Skills

Consonant blends are groups of two or three consonants that are blended together when pronounced, with each consonant being heard in the blend (for example, bl and nd as in blend). Have your child identify the words with consonant blends in the list below. Then help your child find words with consonant blends in this book:

pigs	spiders	dry	dung	desert
insects	bird	snorting	monster	river

Fluency

Fluency is the ability to read accurately with speed and expression. Help your child practice fluency by using one or more of the following activities:

- Reread this book to your child at least two times while he or she uses a finger to track each word as you read it.
- Read the first sentence aloud. Then have your child reread the sentence with you. Continue until you have finished this book.
- Ask your child to read aloud the words they know on each page of this book. (Your child will learn additional words with subsequent readings.)
- Have your child practice reading this book several times to improve accuracy, rate, and expression.

WORD LIST

Astro the Alien uses the 135 words listed below. The words bolded below serve as an introduction to new vocabulary, while the unbolded words are more familiar or frequently used. You may wish to write the words on index cards and use them to help your child build automatic word recognition. Regular practice with these words will enhance your child's fluency in reading connected text.

a	**cactus**	**fast**	I	many	**rain(s)**	**stay**	**warm**
afraid	**camping**	**floods**	**I'd**	**might**	**raining**	stopped	was
alone	can	for	if	**monster**	**rattles**	sun	**watch**
am	come	found	in	**morning**	**rattlesnake**		we
an	**cottontail**	from	**insect(s)**	**mule**	**ready**	**tarantula**	when
and	**coyote**	fun	is		**real**	that	will
animals			it('s)	**nest**	**rising**	the	with
are	dark	get(ting)	its	**night**	river	them	**worry**
asked	**dawn**	**Gila**		no	**roadrunner**	there	**wren**
Astro	deer	go	**jackrabbit**	not		they	
at	**desert**	good			safe	this	you
	did		**leave**	of	said	to	
beetles	does	had	like	oh	saw	**toad**	
Ben	don't	hear(d)	**live**	out	**scared**	today	
bird	**dry**	here	**lizard**	over	see(ing)	too	
bite	**dung**	high	look	owl	**should**	**tortoise**	
bobcat	**dusk**	hot	lot		**so**		
builds		**hunt**	**loud**	**packrat**	some	up	
but	Eva	hurt		**phew**	**something**		
butterfly	even			play	**sometimes**		
	exciting			**pretty**	spider(s)		

ABOUT THE AUTHOR

Emily Sohn is an award-winning journalist in Minneapolis, Minnesota. She writes for many magazines and newspapers and has written dozens of graphic novels and other books for kids. She started her career as the science writer on an expedition team that produced interactive, educational content for a website that was viewed by hundreds of thousands of students in classrooms around the world.

ABOUT THE ILLUSTRATOR

Carlos Aón was born in Buenos Aires, Argentina. He studied in a comic book art academy for four years. In 2000, he graduated as a graphic designer. Aón's work appears in dozens of graphic novels, story books, and educational projects in the United States, Argentina, Europe, and Asia.